D0466237

Libby and Pearl
The Best of Friends

BY LINDSEY BONNICE

HARPER
An Imprint of HarperCollinsPublishers

WITHDRAWN

Some say we're unlikely friends.
They call us a funny pair.

That might seem true.

We look nothing alike.

But we both look amazing in pink

and fierce in a cape.

Together we take on important projects.

We come up with the best plans and schemes.

Some of them work out perfectly.

Others don't.

And a few land us in hot water.

(Which, let's face it, is way more fun.)

We face big decisions.

We have the greatest adventures.

Occasionally, we don't see eye to eye,

since we have different points of view.

We're not always on the same page,

but we're part of each other's story.

Sometimes we're out of step . . .

or out of tune.

Sometimes one of us is up . . .

and the other is down.

It's nothing a best friend can't fix.

A little quality time can work a lot of magic.

So even though we're a funny pair,

we sure know how to laugh,

have fun,

find joy,

and share love.

There's plenty between us, with extra to spare.

To my sweet family and friends who encourage,
love, and support me in all of my dreams!

Libby and Pearl: The Best of Friends
Text copyright © 2016 by Laura Driscoll
Photos copyright © 2016 by Lindsey Bonnice
All rights reserved. Manufactured in China.
No part of this book may be used or reproduced in any manner whatsoever without written
permission except in the case of brief quotations embodied in critical articles and reviews. For
information address HarperCollins Children's Books, a division of HarperCollins Publishers,
195 Broadway, New York, NY 10007.
www.harpercollinschildrens.com

Library of Congress Control Number: 2015956265
ISBN 978-0-06-245927-5

The artist used a Canon 6D SLR camera and an iPhone 6 to create the photos for this book.
Typography by Alison Klapthor
16 17 18 19 20 SCP 10 9 8 7 6 5 4 3 2 1
❖
First Edition

31901060233618